For my son Josha

VIKING
Published by the Penguin Group
Viking Penguin, a division of Penguin Books USA Inc.,
375 Hudson Street, New York, New York 10014, U.S.A.
Penguin Books Australia Ltd, Ringwood, Victoria, Australia
Penguin Books Canada Ltd, 2801 John Street, Markham, Ontario, Canada L3R 1B4
Penguin Books (N.Z.) Ltd, 182-190 Wairu Road, Auckland 10, New Zealand

First published 1991 in Great Britain by ABC, All Books for Children,
a division of the All Children's Company Ltd

First American edition published in 1991

1 3 5 7 9 10 8 6 4 2

Library of Congress Catalog Card Number: 91-50261

ISBN 0-670-84164-1

Printed in Hong Kong

Go Fish

Lucy Dickens

Viking

Herbert didn’t like the water.
He didn’t know how to swim.
He even hated getting his feet wet.

Herbert's mother tried to help. "You'll like it once you're in, Herbert," she coaxed. "Just try."

But the more she tried, the more stubborn Herbert got.

“How will he ever learn
to take care of himself?” cried
his mother. “How will he learn
to catch fish, if he can’t even swim?”

"I don't know what to do," said Herbert's father. "But we'd better go find him some fish while he's playing."

As soon as his parents padded off, Herbert felt hungry.

"Can I please have some
of your fish?" he asked
the penguins, politely.

“Oh, no,” peeped the penguins. “These are for our babies who are too young to fish.” And they waddled past Herbert.

It started to
snow. The cold snow
was wet as it fell on Herbert.
He shivered and his tummy growled.

"I'll go visit my friends the fishermen," Herbert said. "They'll have some fish."

But his friends had
finished their meal of fresh fish.

“We’ll show you how to catch fish without getting your feet wet,” they offered.

Before long, Herbert was sitting by a hole in the ice, with a line into the water.

He was still sitting there one hour later, and he was still hungry.

He was also tired and bored.

"I'll just lie down for a while," he decided. "This rock is nice and warm."

But no sooner had he got comfortable than the rock slid into the water, taking startled Herbert with it.

“I’m wet!” he bubbled.

"I can swim!" Herbert laughed.

"I like the water after all. Just wait until my parents see me now!"